Aunt Truly's Tales

Other books by Laura McHale Holland

Reversible Skirt: A memoir
Resilient Ruin: A memoir of hopes dashed and reclaimed
The Ice Cream Vendor's Song: Flash fiction
Just In Case: Twenty-one bite-sized stories
The Kiminee Dream: A novel

Aunt Truly's Tales

Enchantment for Story Lovers

Laura McHale Holland

WORD
forest

ISBN paperback: 978-0-9829365-9-7
ISBN ebook: 978-1-7336683-4-7
ISBN audiobook: 978-1-7336683-5-4

Library of Congress control number: 2020924360

Book design by Michelle M. White
Art by Anastasia Khmelevska
Author photo by Moira Holland

Dedication

*For Ruth Stotter, who opened a magical door
and invited so many of us in.*

Contents

Introduction

In a place called Windy Wood, snow falls from November through April, modern conveniences are nonexistent and raccoons deliver food to those in need. Travelers who become snowbound there during winter have no way to contact the outside world, but they're not the least bit upset. That's because they're entertained by Aunt Truly, who regales them with stories gathered during a life so long nobody knows how old she really is.

Aunt Truly isn't always at Windy Wood, though. She sometimes takes off on foot, traveling through time and distance to places only she can hear calling to her. Like Santa Claus, she brings presents, but her deliveries come at unexpected times in the form of stories to be savored and passed on.

This little book contains a sampling of stories Aunt Truly told to Carly Mae Foley, a central character in my novel, *The Kiminee Dream.* Carly Mae happened upon Windy Wood while lost, lonesome and far from home after a traumatic experience. Here's an excerpt from the novel that recounts when Carly Mae and Aunt Truly meet:

Carly Mae rubbed goose-bumped arms as she limped along a dirt road so overgrown it was more like a path. She'd been unable to track time passing since she'd limped away from Dusty's truck. And though she'd left Leon Ames behind, she saw his sneering face every time she closed her eyes, felt his gun at her back at the slightest unusual sound, heard his voice when she curled up on the ground at night unable to sleep. She feared every shadow behind a tree was his. Her formerly quick thoughts were hobbled by doubts, and her vision remained blurred, rendering the world like an Impressionist painting.

Ahead, a family of raccoons, one full grown and three juveniles, waddled from the brush alongside the forest, each one clamping an apple in its teeth. First the mother, then the youngsters dropped the fruit in the road and scurried back to the trees. In addition to apples, the raccoons had dropped carrots, peanuts, cabbage and pears in Carly Mae's path several times on her journey.

She was now so thin, two of her could have fit into the T-shirt flapping against her gaunt frame. She trudged to the fruit and bent forward to pick it up. "Thank you," she called, then bit through bitter skin of deep red into crisp, juicy apple. "You know I thought you were rabid the first time I saw you come onto the road. Raccoons just don't do that. But now I wish you'd come out and visit."

The raccoons remained hidden. As the day wore on, gray clouds conquered the sun. Carly Mae approached a creek that dissected the path. She stepped onto a log that served as a bridge. It wobbled. She almost fell in but regained her balance and inched across. The raccoons peered at her through reeds at the bank. Veering from the road was a path lined by fir trees with purple needles like none she'd ever seen. She continued along and reached a clearing, where a weathered house was surrounded by a picket fence broken in several places. She stepped into the open space and was immediately buffeted by strong winds. She hesitated, then continued toward the building. Hanging from a trellis supporting yellow roses still in bloom at the gate was a faded sign with ornate lettering that said, "Welcome to Windy Wood."

As Carly Mae studied the sign, the front door opened. A bent woman dressed in deep purple from her sturdy lace up ankle boots to the bonnet on her head stood in the doorway and called out, "Well, now, don't dawdle. Come on in. I've got some tasty pea soup on the stove."

Carly Mae entered the home, and the raccoons followed.

"Hello babies," the woman of the house said. She ambled to her refrigerator and pulled out a small fish for each masked animal, opened a door off the kitchen and threw the treats down a set of stairs. "Off you go now," she said as the raccoons skittered into the basement. She winked at Carly Mae. "They're like my kids. Been raisin' 'em since I found a pregnant mom wounded in the woods long, long time ago. That's how I knew you was comin'. They've been takin' food to ya, haven't they?"

"How did you know?"

"It happens once in a blue moon. They chirp and spin in circles outside there, and I know it's time to put out extra tidbits. Not too many folks come by these parts. I've been lookin' forward to your company. Snow's a comin' tonight. Lots of it. You got here just in time." The spinster dished out two bowls of soup and placed them on the table, where she'd already set napkins and spoons.

"I've lost track of time, but it's got to be too soon for snow." Carly Mae sat down as wind whistled and rattled the windows.

"It's the first of November. Too soon for snow in most parts, but not here. Winter comes early and stays late in Windy Wood."

Carly Mae took a sip. "Mmm. This is good. Thank you so much . . . um, what's your name?

"Most folks call me Aunt Truly, or they used to. I don't get many visitors these days."

"Pleased to meet you, Aunt Truly. I'm Carly Mae."

"What a lovely name. It rings a bell. Don't know why."

A shiver of hope ran through Carly Mae as she caught Aunt Truly's eye. "Maybe you heard people are looking for me?"

"Hmm. I don't recall, but my memory isn't what it used to be. Somethin' might come to me."

Hope fading, the teen looked down and took another spoonful of soup. "Well, thank you for this meal, anyway. It's really, really good."

"Just a traditional pea soup, I'm afraid. Nothing special. I believe you're just hungry and tired."

"And eager to go home." Carly Mae put down her spoon and looked out the window above the sink. "Wow! It's blowing even harder out there."

"It's one of those, what do you say, anomalies. The clearing's gonna fill with snow tonight. Drifts high as they sky, as they say. There'll be no gettin' out of here probably till springtime."

Carly Mae put her spoon down and frowned. "How do you know?"

"That's just how it always goes in Windy Wood. Don't worry. I've got plenty of food and supplies to get us through."

The home Carly Mae longs to return to is Kiminee, a fictional town where the peculiar and the ordinary meld, and the love flowing between neighbors is an unspoken constant. Since only one of Aunt Truly's stories is revealed in the novel, this collection shares more of the tales she told during that long ago winter.

The Frog Who Wouldn't Budge

When Illini tribes and a smattering of French settlers lived in what is now Illinois and forests and prairie stretched for mile after mile, a trapper built a cabin in remote woods by what he thought was a quiet pond.

Except the pond wasn't quiet. A golden frog that croaked and chuck-chuck-chucked all the time lived there, too. In fact, the little frog had called that pond home for a long, long time.

The amphibian's claim to the pond mattered not to the trapper, who detested the frog sounds. So he stood up tall by the water's edge, puffed up his chest, stomped his feet, waved his arms and yelled, "Go away, frog, before I catch you and eat you up."

The trapper was a fearsome sight, but the little frog wasn't cowed. He went on about his business, croaking and chuck-chuck-chucking the whole time.

The trapper stormed off and returned with a shotgun. "Go away, frog, before I blast you to high heaven," he growled.

But the little frog wasn't cowed. He croaked and chuck-chuck-chucked with pride. Incensed, the trapper aimed and pulled the trigger. Buckshot sprayed everywhere. Some landed on the little frog, giving him spots of deep greenish brown. This bothered him not a whit. He went about his business, croaking and chuck-chuck-chucking away.

The man returned to his cabin, where he sulked and fumed and sulked some more—until a new idea struck. He bent low to the ground and slinked toward the frog inch by inch. It took half the day because he crept so slowly, but at last, the unsuspecting amphibian was within reach.

He lurched, wrapped his fingers around the poor creature and cackled. "I've got you now!" His face contorted into a sinister smile as he reveled in his victory.

But, again, the golden frog that now had green spots wasn't cowed. He wiggled and croaked, jiggled and chuck-chuck-chucked, tickling the man's hand. Flustered, the captor snorted and loosened his grip while his gutsy prey squiggled out and hopped away.

The trapper pursued, but the frog was too fast, so the man gave up and slumped on home. Soon he heard the frog croaking and chuck-chuck-chucking yet again. He went to bed that night fuming about his nemesis. He couldn't sleep one wink.

But in the morning, the man remembered his fish net. He grabbed it and snuck up on the frog again. This time, he captured and held his mark with ease. He pranced off with glee, wondering what to do with the noisy frog, and then it came to him. "Ha! I'l bury you deep, deep in the ground, you little pest." This the man did, certain he'd never hear from the frog again.

At day's end, he celebrated by roasting a rabbit over his fire pit and heating up biscuits and beans to go with it. As night fell, he drifted off to sleep right by the fire, which was still going strong, keeping him nice and warm. Then, as he dreamt of a quiet life by the pond, he was awakened by a barrage of croaking and chuck-chuck-chucking. He shot up, squinting, and realized the assault on his ears was coming from underground—right where he'd buried the frog.

Enraged, he dug up the hole and pulled out his victim. "Ha! You think you're so smart. I'll put an end to you once and for all!"

The poor thing wasn't the least bit golden anymore; he was tan with greenish brown spots, but he remained alive as alive could be—and not the least bit cowed. He croaked and chuck-chuck-chucked away. Blind with fury, the trapper threw the frog into the flames.

There was a sizzle and a pop. Then hundreds of sparks burst out and flew through the air toward the trapper. As each spark landed, it turned into a tan frog with dark spots. Each one croaked and chuck-chuck-chucked in harmony with the others forged in fire.

Those were the ancestors of the leopard frogs living in these parts to this day. As for the trapper, he ran off hollering up a storm, beating away frogs that croaked and chuck-chuck-chucked at his heels. Nobody ever saw him again, not in Illinois anyway.

Milk for Grandma's Coffee

One morning when I was tall as a yardstick and slim as a lamb, I finished my chores and was moping because my big sister wouldn't play with me.

"I've better things to do than waste time with the likes of you," she said, stitching a pillowcase for her hope chest, for she'd just turned twelve and had decided to put aside childish things, which appeared to include me.

I didn't know what to do. I thought I might go visit friends at the farm across the road. They loved to make mud pies with me. But my mother said no to that. So I went to Grandma, who was tilting back and forth in her squeaky rocking chair, and asked her to tell me a story.

"Well, dear child, I'd love to do that, but why don't you tell me a story first?"

"But Grandma, I don't have any stories to tell," I replied.

She squinted and looked me up and down. "Hmm, then why not get me a spot of milk for my coffee?"

I thought for a minute and decided our cow could help with that. "Sure, Grandma, I know just where to go," I said, and took off for the barn. There, I greeted the cow, patted her neck, and asked, "Can you give me a wee bit of milk for Grandma's coffee?"

The bovine nuzzled me, causing me to giggle. Then she said, "Well, dear child, I've already been milked today, but I'd love to help you and can give a little more if you get me some of that sweet, sweet hay I love to chew."

"I'll be happy to do that. I know just where to go."

I ran to the meadow behind the barn and cried out, "Meadow, oh, meadow, can you spare some of your sweet, sweet hay for our cow?"

The meadow replied, "Well, dear child, I'd love to help you, but you'll have to cut it yourself. There are no bales left."

"How will I do that?" I asked.

"With a scythe, of course," the meadow said.

"I'll be happy to do that. I know just where to go." I dashed to my father's toolshed, but there was no scythe. I looked in the barn, in

the house, everywhere I could think of, and could not find a scythe, so I hustled off to the blacksmith to see if he had one.

I arrived out of breath, greeted the blacksmith, who was standing at his anvil, pounding a red hot horseshoe into shape.

He paused, hammer in mid air and said, "Well, dear child, I'd love to help you, but first I'll need a bushel of acorns for my pig, who has a hankerin' for them."

Thinking of the great oak tree on the edge of our farm, I said, "I'll be happy to do that, and I know just where to go." And I was off. When I arrived, I made my request.

The great oak tree replied, "Well, dear child, I'd love to help you, but I can't shake them down myself, and you're far too small to do it. I'll need you to bring me a blustery wind."

I thought of Lake Michigan, the great inland sea, where the wind was always blowing hard. "I can do that. I know just where to go," I said. And off I went again. My journey was long, but well into the afternoon, I arrived, at last, at the great inland sea. There, I made my request. The wind said not a word. It just blew stronger and stronger, lifted me up, up, up, and carried me all the way back to the oak tree, where it shook down all the acorns I needed for the pig.

I thanked the wind, which whistled away while I gathered acorns. I thanked the tree and carried my bounty to the blacksmith, who fed the pig and gave me a scythe. I thanked him and dashed to the meadow, where I cut sweet hay for the cow. I thanked the meadow, ran to the cow and fed her the hay.

She chewed, then mooed and said she was ready to give me milk for Grandma's coffee. I milked the cow, thanked her, and brought a cup of milk to Grandma, who was tilting back and forth in her squeaky rocking chair, just like I'd left her.

"Thank you, dear child. Tell me, how did you get the milk?" She winked and poured a little into her coffee.

So that day I told my very first story of how I got milk for Grandma's coffee. When I was done, she told me story after story. And after that, my sister never brushed me off again because I always had a good tale to tell. 🌰

The Seamstress

Kaskaskia, a tiny town in Illinois, was once a thriving metropolis—the largest in the region in the 18th century. It was ideally situated for trade on the Mississippi and surrounded by rich agricultural land, so people were drawn to it from all over.

Sadly, a young widow in Kaskaskia was in despair, for like Old Mother Hubbard, she had no food in her cupboard, and she feared her children would starve. But then she remembered her neighbors had always complimented her skills as a seamstress. Some had even begged her to make clothing for them. So she hung out her shingle and began taking orders.

Soon word spread of the charming yet practical clothes she made, and orders flowed in. Her clients didn't pay particularly well, but she was able to support her children, so she was happy. But then her own cape became threadbare, and she couldn't afford to buy material for a new one.

She was concerned about this until she realized one day that if she set aside scraps from her many orders, she'd eventually have enough to make her cape. And so she did. She made a magnificent cape that reached all the way to her ankles. She loved that cape and wore it, wore it, wore it and wore it until it was entirely worn out and altogether useless—so she thought. But then she examined it and saw she had enough material to make a jacket.

So she did. Hers was a spiffy jacket. She loved it just as much as the cape and wore it, wore it, wore it and wore it until it was completely worn out and altogether useless—so she thought. But then she scrutinized it and saw she had enough to make an apron.

So she did. Hers was an appealing apron. She loved that apron just as much as the jacket and wore it, wore it, wore it and wore it until it fully wore out and altogether useless.—so she thought But then she assessed that apron and saw she had enough to make a scarf.

So she did. Hers was a scrumptious scarf. She loved that scarf just as much as the apron, and wore it, wore it, wore it and wore it until it

was totally worn out and altogether useless—so she thought. But then she inspected it and saw she had enough to make a cap.

So she did. Hers was a handsome cap. She loved that cap as much as the scarf and wore it, wore it, wore it and wore it until it was absolutely worn out and altogether useless—so she thought. But then she took the cap apart and saw she had enough to make a button.

So she did. Hers was a beautiful button. She loved that button just as much as the headband. She sewed it on her blouse, and wore it, wore it, wore it and wore it until it was downright worn out and altogether useless—so she thought. But then she took a good, long look and saw she had enough to make a story.

And the story never wore out.

The Diamond

Once on a time, and what a time it was, a handyman traveled from town to town and farm to farm, helping folks repair leaky roofs, paint fences, shore up retaining walls and tend to other pressing tasks. He visited the same communities in the same rotation year after year, and folks anticipated his arrival the same way they looked forward to holidays and birthdays. They were delighted to give him room, board and some cash for his work, and they were invariably disappointed when it was time for him to move on.

One morning after looking skyward to reflect on his good fortune, the handyman considered the best way to fix a broken spoke when he heard the canter of an approaching horse. Soon, a young man yanked his steed to a stop, jumped off and rushed to the worker.

"I know you've got it. Where is it?" the young man demanded.

The handyman pressed fingertips to his temple and asked, "Where is what?"

"I dreamt last night that if I came to this very farm, I'd meet a wise man fixing a wagon wheel who would give me a diamond, a huge diamond. You're the only one here, and it looks like you're about to fix that thing, so you must be the one."

"Ah," the handyman said. He bent down and rifled through his toolbox, which was already open at his feet, and pulled out a sparkling diamond roughly the size of a hockey puck. "Here you go," he said, and handed it over with ease.

The youth accepted the gemstone with a gasp. "Why it's true! It's really true!" he exclaimed before mounting his horse and galloping to a nearby town, where he lived with his parents above a general store they owned.

Once home, he bounded into his bedroom, put the treasure on his dresser and tried to get some rest before reporting to work downstairs. But it was no use. He couldn't stop staring at the diamond, so worried was he that if he closed his eyes, the treasure would be gone when he opened them. Then, there came a knock on his door. It was his mother.

"Come have some breakfast, dear, before you start work," she said.

He stuffed the diamond in his pants pocket and went to the kitchen, where his mom gave him a plate of biscuits and gravy. He continuously tapped his pocket and pushed the food around his plate with his fork. He couldn't eat a bite.

"What's wrong with you, son? You usually have your plate cleaned before I even pour myself a cup of coffee."

"I'm okay, Ma. I'm just not hungry. I'll have a bite later on with Dad."

He went downstairs and, as he stocked shelves, he couldn't stop patting his pants, so worried was he that someone might pick his pocket. He did it so much, in fact, that people noticed.

"What are you so jittery about?" his dad asked him.

He insisted he was fine, but he knew he wasn't, because his voice was shaky and his hands trembled while he wrapped up a neighbor's purchase of salt pork.

"What's wrong with your lad, there?" the neighbor asked. "He's shaking like a leaf."

"That's a right good question," his dad said, eyeing his son with suspicion.

Throughout the morning, the youth's strange behavior escalated. He jumped when the bell jangled as the front door opened. He dropped a teapot when lifting it out of a display case. It shattered on the floor. Later, his hands were so jittery at the candy counter, he couldn't fill a small bag of treats for a child. Finally, when sweat slid from his forehead, down his nose and splashed on a bolt of fabric a woman had just set on the counter, his father apologized to the customer and ordered his son to take the afternoon off.

He gladly ran upstairs and shut himself in his room, where he pulled the diamond from his pocket and put it back on his dresser. For the rest of that day and all through the night, he stared at the sparkling stone, so worried was he that it would disappear in a wink.

At dawn, he returned to the farm and found the handyman already trimming a hedge. "Here, take this away. I don't want it." He held the diamond under the man's nose.

The wise man put down his shears and accepted the gem.

Immediately, the youth chuckled with relief. "Whew! I'm glad to be rid of that thing. I don't want it anymore."

"Why is that?"

"What do you know that made it so easy for you to part with it like it was just some pebble or a stick? That's what I want to know, too."

The Wee Woman Who Lived in a Teapot

Once there was not and then there was a wee woman who lived in a teapot. She was most unhappy with her abode. Every day she rocked back and forth upon an old tree stump outside her door and grumbled. "Oh what a sorrow, a deep abiding sorrow that I should live in a teapot. It doesn't even have a bathroom and it's hot as hades inside. Plus, there is no store around for miles. I deserve to live in a little flat with indoor plumbing in a nice neighborhood with all the things I need nearby."

One day a kindly fairy, who was flitting here and there looking for a good deed to do, heard the woman's complaint. Taking pity upon her, she flew over and said, "When you're ready for the sandman tonight, turn around three times, climb under the covers, close your eyes, and don't open them till morning. Then you'll be in for a great big surprise."

So, all set for sleep that evening, the wee woman turned around three times, climbed under the covers, closed her eyes and fell fast asleep in her teapot. In the morning, she awoke in a fully furnished flat with indoor plumbing. The neighborhood was bustling. A commercial street was two short blocks away. It had a general store, pharmacy, gift shop, coffee shop, library and much more.

A few weeks later, the fairy stopped by the wee woman's flat. "Surely she'll be happy now," the fairy thought. But as she approached, she saw the woman, sitting on a folding chair on the sidewalk outside her building. And what was the woman doing? Grumbling.

"Oh, what a sorrow, a deep, abiding sorrow, that I should live in this cramped old flat. The landlord raised the rent yesterday, the faucets leak and my upstairs neighbors dance every night away. I deserve to own cottage in a quiet neighborhood, with a nice yard to comfort me. That's what I deserve."

The kindly fairy took pity upon her again, and said, "When you're ready for the sandman tonight, turn around three times, climb under the covers, close your eyes, and don't open them till morning. Then you'll have a great big surprise."

The wee woman followed the fairy's instructions, and in the morning, she awoke in a lovely cottage. It had two bedrooms, and a beautifully landscaped yard that included a rose garden and gazebo. The neighborhood was quiet but still within walking distance of everything she needed.

A few weeks later, the fairy stopped by the wee woman's new home. "Surely she'll be happy now," the fairy thought. But as she approached, she saw the woman, sitting in a rocking chair on her porch. And what was she doing? Grumbling.

"Oh, what a sorrow, a deep, abiding sorrow, that I should live in a musty old cottage. The roof leaks, the front steps are cracked, the neighbors's things are finer than mine, and I can't possibly take care of the place without help. I deserve my very own mansion with spacious grounds, five bedrooms, all the latest amenities so I can entertain guests properly, quarters for servants to serve my meals and maintain the home, and a chauffeur to drive me wherever I need to go."

The kindly fairy was surprised, but once again, she took pity upon the wee woman, and said, "Just before the sandman comes tonight, turn around three times, climb under the covers, close your eyes, and don't open them till morning. Then you'll have a great big surprise."

The wee woman followed the instructions, and the next morning, she awoke in her dream mansion, with servants on every floor and a chauffeur at the curb waiting to drive her wherever she wished.

A few weeks later, the fairy stopped by the wee woman's new abode. "Surely she'll be happy now," the fairy thought. But as she approached, she saw the woman sitting on a swing on her spacious front porch. And what was the woman doing? Grumbling.

"Oh, what a sorrow, a deep, abiding sorrow, that I should live in a mere mansion. I should be a queen living in a castle with everyone bowing down to me and offering patronage of all kinds. I should have sonnets written extolling my beauty, parades on my birthday, and visits from heads of state worldwide. That's what I deserve.

A little saddened, the kindly fairy took action once again, "Right before the sandman comes tonight, turn around three times, climb under the covers, close your eyes, and keep them closed till morning. Then you'll have a great big surprise."

So the wee woman did just what the fairy said. In the morning, she awoke. And where was she? Right back in the teapot.

"And that's where she'll remain," the fairy said, "because if she can't be happy in her teapot, she won't be happy anywhere else."

Hidden Skin

Longer than a long time ago, when I was on the cusp of womanhood, my mother and I journeyed to Prince Edward Island, where she was born and raised. It was a chance for me to meet my grandparents and other relatives, and since our roots went all the way back to the first Irish who settled there, I hoped to learn a little family lore. I must say, though, my own kin were stubbornly closed-mouthed about the past. But that matters not a whit now.

While there, I saw a young man at a barn party. He was handsome, but his eyes were so very sad. I inquired about him, but everyone said I should steer clear because he wasn't right in the head.

"That's crazy Owen Lavelle," my cousin Bernadette said.

"What do you mean? He doesn't look crazy to me," I said.

And then she told me he was orphaned as a lad in Ireland, and his uncle, James, sent for him and raised him as his own. The story went that his mum drowned and his dad had died of a broken heart shortly thereafter. Owen never said anything different, so everyone assumed it was true. He had this quiet sort of appeal, and lots of young women tittered over him when he got to be of marrying age. Since he was a little shy, his uncle, who was a prosperous farmer, arranged a visit with Susan Bright, a young lady from a prominent family. The two appeared to be a good match, and soon he was courting her in earnest. However, on a visit one afternoon, he said he could not in good conscience ask for her hand in marriage without telling her the truth about his parents.

Curious, Susan was all ears as he told her his father, Seamus Lavelle, was a fisherman on the Atlantic coast of County Mayo, doing well in most respects, except he'd been unlucky in love. Then one afternoon, he was walking the beach, feeling desperately alone, when he heard the most beautiful song and enchanting laughter coming from the other side of an outcropping of rock just ahead. He snuck up and peeked around the rock formation and saw five beautiful women dancing on the shore. To the side and quite near his perch were five seal skins. Seamus knew right away they were selkies, the mystical creatures who lived in the sea as seals but could come ashore, shed their skins and become beautiful women who enjoyed the occasional afternoon reveling on dry land.

At that moment, Owen's sweetheart, greatly agitated, opened her fan and waved it vigorously, though the afternoon was not the least bit hot. "Good gracious!" she interjected. "What sort of story are you tellin' me?"

"I do not mean to alarm you, but I must get this out, love," he said.

"All right, then, if you must. But Selkies? You've got to be pullin' my leg."

Owen assured her he wasn't fibbing and continued his story. He said his very own father, on impulse, reached out and took one of the skins, ran to his lonely little cottage, locked the skin in a wooden chest, and slipped the key into his pocket. When he returned to the shore, one young woman sat shivering on the sand, watching her friends, returned to seal form, swimming away. He asked the maiden what was wrong. With tears streaming down her perfect face, she said, "I've lost my sealskin, and now I can't go home with my family."

Seamus peeled off his jacket and handed it to her to shelter her from the wind, and suggested perhaps the skin had blown away and they should look for it. Of course, they didn't find the skin, and as the day drew to a close, he invited her to his cottage. One thing led to another, and soon they married. In town, folks asked where the girl had come from, and Seamus was vague, just saying she'd come from up north, which seemed enough to satisfy everyone.

It wasn't long before they had two sons and a daughter and seemed as happy as any other family. Occasionally, the young mother would inquire about the box, but Seamus said it just held some old clothes, and he'd lost the key long ago. Then one day, he had to take care of business in town, and he tripped going out the door. His wife saw something fall from his pocket, and as she went to help him up, she grabbed the key and put it in her apron pocket. Flummoxed by his fall, Seamus didn't notice anything amiss.

Later, with her husband away and children outside playing, she tried the key in the chest's lock. It worked! And when she lifted the lid she saw her sealskin inside. The urge to put it on was so strong, she raced to the shore, giving her offspring only one quick wave before she put it on and dove into the sea. All three children dove in after her. Farther and farther they went, but they couldn't catch her. Their father returned just as waves overwhelmed his brood He tried to save all three, but in the end, Owen was the only one he was able to bring ashore.

Full of sorrow and regret that night, Seamus confessed to his only surviving son how he'd stolen the sealskin and had no right to do so. In the following months, he stopped working, and drank homemade

spirits day and night, which led to his death. That is when James Lavelle sent for Owen. And when the lad arrived, James told him to never speak of his family's fate in Ireland, and he never had until that very moment.

With the story told, the young man felt he could start his new life, but Susan didn't see it that way.

"You're a crazy one, you are, Owen Lavelle." She pulled away from him. "I'll not marry someone who thinks such daft things. How can you even set foot in a church believing such wicked pagan nonsense?"

With that, she stood abruptly and raced away. Not only that, she warned all her friends about him, exaggerating details, saying he himself said he was a shapeshifter who became a sea monster that devoured cod and herring in the night, making the fish they depended on scarce. This, or course, was not true. He didn't inherit the gift of shapeshifting, nor did he have an ounce of evil in his bones. But people on the island believed her, and no young woman in the vicinity was willing to marry him. As an outsider who'd witnessed plenty of unusual things in my short life thus far, I wasn't put off by the notion of shapeshifting. I figured all of us must have had some of it in our heritage if you go back far enough. I was drawn to Owen even more.

As our time on Prince Edward Island came to a close, I told my mum I wanted to visit Owen, and she said that would be fine. So we called on the Lavelles, and she visited with his uncle, while Owen and I took a walk in their garden. I mentioned the story I'd heard about his mother, and he took my hands, looked into my eyes, and said, "It's true. I swear it. I was there, for part of it, anyway."

I knew from the look in his eyes that he was telling the truth. I also knew he wasn't crazy like everyone thought. "I believe I've found a kindred spirit," I said as my heart swelled with love. Without needing to say another word, we both knew we were meant for each other.

When we returned to his uncle's home, he asked my mother for my hand in marriage. She said she'd consult with my father when we returned home and send word to him of our answer. My father had no objection, and soon Owen and I were married in Illinois far from Prince Edward Island and all the judgments people made about him.

We had countless happy times together at our homestead, Windy Wood, which has some quirks that don't exactly follow the usual physical laws. Nobody ever gave us trouble over that in these parts though. In fact, they thought of our home as a healing sort of place and often came to stay for a few days if they ever felt depleted. My Owen passed long ago, but I love him now just as much as the day he asked for my hand in marriage. And my Windy Wood is still a healing sort of place.

Crimson

Long ago, but not too far away, a family of cardinals lived in a verdant forest. The mother sported light brown plumage with reddish crest, wings and tail. The father was brilliant red. Both had black masks. Two brown babies, a boy they named Carnelian and a girl named Caramel, peeped in triumph after pecking through their shells. A third had yet to hatch. Hovering over their nest high up in a dogwood tree, the parents listened for tapping sounds while they waited–and waited–and waited.

After a week went by, the father said, "We have a fine family now. Let's worry no more over this last one."

The mother wouldn't have it. "I can't let our little one go. I simply can't."

Carnelian and Caramel wished the egg would disappear, because every moment their parents spent worrying about the one who refused to emerge was time they weren't gathering food.

The days wore on. The father grew restless, the youngsters resentful, the mother resolute. Finally, the teeny, tiniest baby poked through his shell.

The mother puffed up with pride. "Ah, a boy. Let's call him Crimson."

The father agreed, patting the fuzzy brown tyke with his coral-colored beak. However, he and his mate worried because the final offspring was way too small and far too thin. To help him bulk up, they gave him extra bits of food, often the best parts of the bugs and such that they brought to the nest.

This did not sit well with Carnelian and Caramel. So they came up with a plan.

One day, both parents went hunting after a light rain. Carnelian maneuvered to the edge of the nest and looked toward the horizon. "Wow. A rainbow. What a glorious sight!"

"Lemme see, lemme see." Caramel wiggled over by her big brother, craned her neck toward the horizon and exclaimed, "Oh, my, it is a rainbow! A truly glorious sight!"

Crimson wanted to see, too, so he squeezed in next to his siblings, stretched his neck as far as he could, but saw only the side of the nest and a few branches directly above. "Phooey," he said. "I guess I'll have to miss it. What does it look like? Is it big? Is it wide as the sky? Can you tell me?"

"I'll do better than that," Carnelian said. "I'll lift you up here, and you'll see for yourself."

Envisioning brilliant colors in the sky, Crimson agreed. His brother perched him on the edge of the nest, but he saw only trees, blue sky and a few fluffy white clouds. "I don't see a rainbow," he said.

"Lean out farther, and you will," Caramel said.

Crimson stretched and stretched, but he saw no rainbow.

"Farther," the brother cried out.

Crimson balanced himself precariously on the edge. "Where is it?" he asked.

Instead of answering, the brother and sister both gave him a big shove, and over the edge he tumbled down, down, down. Not yet able to fly, he was about to smash into the ground when a gust of wind carried him off. He was too stunned to make a peep.

Carnelian and Caramel were pleased with themselves, that is, until their providers returned to find Crimson missing. Aghast, they asked what had happened. Brother and sister insisted he'd fallen out by accident. The mom and dad searched the underbrush, along hidden forest paths, on low-hanging branches and even in mud puddles and ponds for their third child, but it was no use. They returned to the nest resigned that their youngest was lost. Seeing sorrow on their parents' faces made the two tricksters regret their treachery, but, alas, they couldn't undo their deed.

Meanwhile, Crimson came to a stop in unfamiliar terrain. By then it was dark and cold. Terrified and feeling sorry for himself, he wept. The sound carried to a fox, who perked up her ears and padded toward the snuffles and peeps of distress.

"What is your trouble, little one?" the predator asked as she drew close.

"I'm lost and don't know how to get home," Crimson blubbered.

"Oh, I can take you there." The fox pointed her nose toward the river. "You live just on the other side. Hop on my back, and you'll be home in a jiffy."

So, Crimson hopped on the fox's back, and into the river they went. But when they reached the other side, the fox said, "I hope you don't mind. I have to feed my children before I take you home."

Without waiting for an answer, the fox dashed to her den. Crimson held tightly to her fur with his tiny talons. When they arrived she told Crimson to hop off and wait by the door while she woke up her kits. It was windy though, so Crimson followed instead of doing what he was told. It was a good thing, too, because he overheard her whisper to her young. "I have a wee and wonderful morsel for you, waiting at the door," she said. "He thinks I'm taking him home. Ha!"

At this, Crimson hustled out of the den and into the cold, cold wood. He found a crevice in a boulder and squeezed inside. The fox chased him and scratched at the hole but soon gave up on capturing him and went in search of more promising prey.

Crimson trembled all night long. When the morning sun blazed into the crevice, he woke up consumed by hunger. He stuck his eye to the hole and saw an enormous feathered being. Terrified, he pulled back, drawing a deep breath.

"Hello in there. What brings you here?" the beast called.

"I'm hiding from the fox who promised to take me home but wanted to feed me to her kits instead."

"How terrible! I would never dream of doing something like that."

"How can I be sure?"

"I'm a majestic eagle. The bravest of the brave, best of the best. Are you yourself not a bird?"

"Yes, I'm Crimson, a cardinal."

"Ah, cardinals. Beautiful birds. I would never wish to harm someone like you. Come closer, have a good look at me, see how friendly I am."

Trembling, the hungry fledgling poked his head out just as the eagle spied a worm in the black earth, grabbed it and offered it to him. Crimson gobbled it up.

"Why not come out here so I can get a good look at you?" the eagle asked.

"But your claws are so big and sharp."

"The better to carry you back to your family, my dear."

"You know where I live?"

"It's not that far. Let me take you home."

Wary, Crimson demurred and withdrew into his shelter.

"Suit yourself. My babies have just hatched, and I must take care of them. You'll wither away in that rock, poor thing." She stretched out her massive wings.

Thoughts of starvation filled Crimson with dread, so he hopped out of his shelter and cried out, "Wait! Wait! I'm coming!"

The eagle grabbed him in her claws, and up, up they flew.

But instead of taking him home as promised, the eagle spirited Crimson to her own nest. "Look, my babies, food for you," the eagle crowed as she hovered over her brood and let go of her prey.

As he plummeted toward the nest, which was high, high up an outcropping of rock jutting skyward, Crimson froze in fear. But the moment his feet touched the squalling eaglets, he jumped with all his might, and sprang up to the edge of the nest. There, with the babies lurching for him, he propelled himself away. Down, down he plunged, along with one of the eaglets that had given chase. The mother eagle dove to save her own child. And just as she carried the eaglet back in the nest, Crimson fell smack into the net of a boy who'd been on the hunt for butterflies.

"Whoa! What have we here?" the boy exclaimed.

Winded, Crimson managed to eek out a question, "Can you help me get home?"

Thrilled with his catch, the boy said, "Oh, I'll get you home all right." And ran straight to his mother and father. "Can we keep him? Can we keep him?" he begged.

"Please let me go," Crimson cried out.

Seeing the sparkle in their son's eyes, the parents ignored the cardinal. They found an old birdcage in their attic, cleaned it up and put him inside. "He'll be the talk of the town one day," the mother predicted. The father agreed.

But Crimson was miserable behind bars. His captors fed him well, and he grew into a strong bird that was brilliant red just as the parents had expected. They showed him off to anyone and everyone who came to visit. He was poked, prodded and insulted for being unfriendly. He remained silent and sullen as they peered into his cage.

The months wore on. Fearing he'd never get home, he came up with a scheme at last. From then on, he danced in his cage when the boy came into the room. He greeted the lad warmly, asked questions about his day, even laughed at his awful jokes. It wasn't long before the boy was taking Crimson out of the cage and letting the bird perch on his shoulder for a little while every afternoon.

Then one day when the mom was doing spring cleaning and all the windows were open to air out the home, the boy entered the room.

"You are the best boy ever," Crimson said. "I don't know why I ever feared you."

"Why thank you," the boy replied. "It's about time you appreciated all that we've done for you. He opened Crimson's cage to add some fresh seed.

Crimson hopped on his hand, hoping the boy would take him out to perch on his shoulder, but the boy shook him off.

"Not today, the windows are open. You might fly away," the boy said.

"I would never ever do that. I know I could not make it on my own in the wild."

"You're right about that."

"The fresh air smells so beautiful, though. I really would like to peek outside."

"Oh, yes, it is beautiful outside. Trees are budding and flowers are blooming. It's quite a sight."

"Could you show me?" Crimson asked.

"I probably shouldn't," the boy replied.

"Please, please, I really would like to see just for a moment."

"Well, okay." The boy held his hand for Crimson to hop on. And as soon as the boy pulled his arm from the cage, Crimson skittered across the room and hopped onto the window sill.

"Come back here!" The boy rushed toward the bird.

Crimson didn't look back. Just as the boy was about to grab him, he leapt out the window. Heart thumping, he flapped his wings, fearing he'd fall straight to the ground, but he was amazed as his wings took him higher and higher.

The boy called out as the bird flew up and away. "You'll never survive. Come to your senses, you ungrateful bird!"

Crimson gave the words no thought as he dipped and twirled and spun in the air. Higher, higher he soared over field and meadow, forest and glade until he smelled something familiar. The scent of the forest he once called home. He looked for signs of his family but found none, which made him feel lonesome and despondent. But then on the wind, came the most glorious song the young cardinal had ever heard. Swiftly, the sound flushed out all of his despair.

Crimson raced toward the song. Then, on a blooming dogwood branch, he saw a lovely bird, not part of his lost family, but still very much the same. Her warm brown feathers with red tinges in her wings, tail and crest were divine. Her red beak magnificent, black face a thing of beauty. He landed a couple feet away from her and sang to her, a song he didn't know was inside of him. And their duet soared as they inched toward each other.

And so it was. They lived long and raised many young, none of whom was ever pushed out of the nest.

Taken

Not so very long ago, in the deep of an Irish night, a farmer near Fermoy sat in the shadows of his kitchen, waiting. While his family slept, he was in the dark, listening.

Then through the door came an extraordinary young woman. She had long flowing hair shining in a glint of moonlight, fine features, the most beautiful he'd ever seen. She walked gracefully to his table, lifted a bowl of milk to her lips and drank it all. Then she turned and headed for the door, and the farmer rose and stepped into her path.

"Who are you, and why have you been coming here in the night, taking any food and drink we might happen to leave out?" He demanded.

She pointed to the empty bowl. "That was all I wanted."

"It seems we've been feeding you for quite a long time. I deserve more of an explanation than that, lass."

Her bottom lip quivered, and she swayed, losing her balance. The farmer took her arm, brought her back to the table, and sat down with her. "There now, it can't be that bad. Come, tell me. Go on now. Tell me."

She replied in song:

> I was a lass in Ventry parish and there I married a lad
> We farmed the land workin' hand in hand
> But in less than a year things turned bad
>
> For I grew ill consumed by fever and coughin' night and day
> Twas a sorry plight, none could set me right
> And I saw death a comin' my way
>
> On my own, am I; all alone, I cry
> Will no one rescue me?
>
> I begged my man to tell my parents to come and take me home
> For I longed to be with my family
> near the hills I could never more roam

At the hearth I lay and my dear mother sat close throughout the night
She is not to blame that her skirt caught flame
At the moment the faeries took flight

On my own, am I; all alone, I cry
Will no one rescue me?

They carried me right here to Fermoy and now I know only strife
I refuse their bread for I know it's said
If I do I'll be theirs all my life

So I sneak outside when right at midnight the faeries dance and play
And your food I eat but then retreat
If they caught me I'd dearly pay

On my own, am I; all alone, I cry
Will no one rescue me?

So I beg you now to write my people and tell them where I dwell
They're named O'Shea; they must find a way
To get me released from this hell

On my own, am I, all alone, I cry
Will no one rescue me?

Her appeal finished, the woman looked down at her lap.

The farmer put a hand on her arm, cleared his throat and said, "I'll write you that letter, dear."

She looked up, eyes wide with hope. "Be sure to tell my mother about the fire. She'll remember that and know it really is me that needs her now. She'll know the faeries replaced me with a dying changeling."

She then returned to the faeries, for they let down their guard only at midnight and only for a short time. It was then she would slip away from their fort, called a liss, but she could walk only a short distance. It was as though they had her leashed, and on her own, she could not break their spell.

The farmer wrote the letter to the O'Sheas in Ventry parish and put a seal on it to show how important it was. When the parents read the letter, they were beside themselves. They didn't know what to do. They didn't even know if they should tell her husband. They were ashamed they hadn't realized the faeries had taken their daughter and replaced her with a dying changeling. And her husband had re-married after a respectable period of mourning. Now he and his new wife had two children. The O'Sheas were so distraught, all they did was keen at the impostor's grave and curse the faeries every day.

But the beautiful young woman kept returning to the farmer in Fermoy, and he kept writing letters for her. The O'Sheas finally told the husband about the situation. He was deeply troubled and sought advice from his friends. Soon all the neighbors knew, and throughout the parish, people talked about how it didn't seem right to leave the stolen wife in the liss with the faeries.

Finally, after the seventh letter, the husband, mother and father determined they must fetch her. Along the way, in Dingle, they noticed a church near the road. They stopped in to ask the priest for advice on how to go about the rescue.

He listened with much compassion as their feelings poured out. But then he said to the husband, "Ah, this is a hard case, very hard, but you know, lad, it's not right for a man to have two wives. It would cause upset throughout the countryside."

"Oh, I wasn't planning to bring her back to Ventry parish, Father," the husband replied. "We can send her to relatives in America. She can start a new life there."

"I'm sorry, son, but no matter where in the world she is, she would still be your wife. So you see, it would be a greater evil for you to go against the Pope than to let your wife live out her days with the faeries, eating their bread. The faeries are not of this world, you see."

The mother, father and husband felt great sorrow at this, torn between the church they relied upon cradle to grave and their love for their precious girl. They talked and prayed for hours, but they found no way around what the priest said. So with slow steps and heavy hearts, they reversed course and went home.

The mother wrote a letter to the farmer in Fermoy telling him that it broke their hearts, but they were not coming, and she told him why. When the farmer received the letter, he left it on the table, beside a bowl of milk. Then in the deep of that night, the breathtaking beauty walked in, picked up the letter, read it and put it in her skirt pocket. Ignoring the milk, she turned and walked out the farmer's door.

He heard her singing as she slipped away:

> *On my own, am I; all alone, I cry*
> *No one will rescue me*

Back in the liss, the faeries offered her a piece of bread, and for the first time she accepted it. She brought it to her lips, bit into the sweet, savory crust, and smiled.

The Mermaid's Gift

When the world's magic flowed freely on fresh morning winds, when it danced through meadows of wild flowers, when it flowed like a river from heart to heart; back then, on the moon-lit coast of Brittany, mermaids came to shore to comb their shimmering hair.

These sirens of the sea loved treasures: strings of pearls, golden earrings, silver bracelets studded with precious stones, jewels of every size, color and shape. They found them all at the very bottom of the sea in sunken ships lost to humankind long ago.

They liked to see treasures gleam in the sunlight, too. So on rare and balmy afternoons, they would come ashore and spread their riches out on snow-white tablecloths in the sand. But if a human

should happen upon them, they would quickly gather up their valu-
ables and dive back into the sea.

One day, two little girls, Clarisse and Celestine, frolicked, collect-
ing shells on the beach. They found many unusual shells that day,
and they went farther and farther in search of more until they heard
a strange yet beautiful song.

> *Oh treasures lovely to see*
> *Sparkle as a heart so true*
> *Oh, bounty lost and set free*
> *Trust in wishes old as new*

Enchanted, they marched toward the voice. Closer and closer they
drew until they came upon a mermaid admiring her belongings as
she sang that beguiling song. The mermaid was so absorbed, she did
not notice the girls, who crept up, barely breathing, step by tiny step,
until they were inches from the cloth.

Then Clarisse stumbled and gasped as she regained her balance.
The mermaid looked up, clutching a silver brooch. Frightened, the
girls stepped back.

But the mermaid's eyes shone kindly upon them, and instead of
gathering her things and diving back into the sea, she smiled and

motioned for them to come closer. "Don't be afraid, little ones. I was once a child, too. Come. I have gifts for you."

Both girls inched forward, trembling. "Please don't hurt us," Celestine said.

"We didn't mean to intrude," Clarisse added.

"Don't be silly. Come closer. I want to give each of you a present. Wouldn't you like that?"

The mermaid's smile was so wide and her eyes so sincere, the girls relaxed and leaned in as she filled two linen napkins and knotted them closed so swiftly, the girls had no idea what was inside. She handed a napkin to Celestine, and said, "Tuck this into your pocket, and take it home. Do not open it along the way. Wait until you're with your parents."

"Oh thank you, thank you. I will," Celestine said as she accepted the gift and tucked it into her coat pocket.

The mermaid then gave Clarisse her gift with the same instruction. Clarisse also thanked the mermaid and assured her she would do as told.

Satisfied, the mermaid gave the friends one last smile and waved them off. "Go now. Go home. And heed what I said."

The girls trotted off, but soon paused to look back just in time to see the mermaid's tail disappear into the waves. The companions scampered away. For a time, they were in high spirits, laughing and playing, but as the afternoon wore on, they slowed to a trudge because they were tired and had wandered far from home. Bored and restless, Celestine rubbed the cloth in her pocket again and again.

Finally, she stopped and took the napkin out. "I want to see what the beautiful mermaid gave me. Don't you?"

"Of course I do," Clarisse replied.

"Let's open them now then," Celestine urged. "Why wait until we get home. A gift's a gift wherever it is."

"Yes, but the mermaid told us to wait until we were home."

"I don't care. I can't wait!" Celestine plopped on a driftwood log, undid the knot, and pulled the napkin open. Inside was nothing but sand. "Why, that nasty creature tricked us. It's just the same as the sand under our feet. It's worthless," she complained. She threw the cloth into the sea. "You ought to just throw yours away too. Go ahead open it. It's nothing but sand."

"Maybe so, but I'm going to wait," Clarisse said, tempted though she was.

So the girls plodded on and parted ways when they reached their village, one girl going home empty handed, the other walking inside her house with a knotted linen cloth in her pocket.

"I met a mermaid today," Clarisse told her family.

"Sure, and I caught a golden fish," he father teased.

Her mother and brother laughed. Unfazed, she put the napkin on the table. And as her family gathered around, she told them about the mermaid and the gift that now rested on the table. And she told them of Celestine's disappointment on the way home.

"It's probably just sand," Clarisse said. Hoping she was wrong, she loosened the knot and opened the napkin.

For a moment, mother, father, sister and brother were speechless, for before their eyes was a mix of jewels more precious than they'd ever imagined.

It is said they used their treasure wisely and thereafter always had more than enough. But who can say? It was so long ago that magic flowed freely on fresh morning winds.

The Snow Girl

Once long ago and so far back in time that my great, great, great grandmother wasn't even a twinkle in her mother's eye, a boy named Roddy and a girl named Rosalyn fell deeply in love. And when they came of age, they married and made for one another a warm and cozy home.

They worked hard through the seasons and were generous with their neighbors, sharing bounty from their fields in the summer and preserves from their cellar in winter. Each month, they prayed for a child, but again and again, they were disappointed. As the years passed, their hearts grew heavier with each wrinkle and every gray hair, knowing their childbearing years were coming to an end.

Seeing Roddy and Roslyn's grief, some folks avoided them, clueless about what to do. Some even whispered that the couple must have done something evil to deserve being barren. But plenty of villagers stood by them, knowing misfortune hits us all in different ways.

So it was one winter's day that Roddy was on his way home after enjoying a good smoke and story swap with a neighbor when a moist snow danced down from the heavens. Roddy stopped when he saw children shaping a drift into a large ball to form the base of a snowman. A joy he hadn't felt in decades filled his heart when he heard their laughter. Then, struck with an idea, he broke into a run.

"Rosalyn, love," he called when he reached his front porch. "Come outside, and hurry up. A perfect snow is falling."

Rosalyn untied her apron, threw it over a chair, put on her coat and scarf and rushed out the door. There she saw her husband grinning with his hands clasped at his chest.

"Whatever has you so excited?" she asked.

"Let's make a snow child. Right now. A beautiful snow child. Boy or girl. I don't care."

Rosalyn took a fancy to the idea and immediately pulled her mittens from her pocket and put them on. "Yes! A snow child—a snow child of our very own. Let's get to work."

So they rolled and packed and shaped the snow with the tenderness of new parents doting on a baby. As they worked, word spread around the village that Roddy and Rosalyn were up to something peculiar, and a crowd gathered, curious about what was going on. Soon they saw a child emerge, a beautiful girl the likes of which no one had ever seen. She was perfectly proportioned from head to toe.

Detractors snickered and said the old geezers had lost their marbles. Most, however, were enthralled with what a short time ago was merely a big lump of snow. Roddy and Rosalyn clothed the child in a cousin's hand-me-downs, which made her look quite real, and finally, they patted two coals into place for her eyes. The moment they stepped back to view their creation, the snow girl came to life and sprang forward to embrace them.

"Oh, Mommy, Daddy, thank you so much! At last I am whole and have a family of my own." Her voice was mellifluous and enchanting.

Roddy and Rosalyn named their daughter Melody, and all through the winter the days passed merrily. She often played with other children, who had no trouble accepting her. It was as if she'd always been part of their lives.

But as the days grew longer and winter gradually melted into spring, the snow girl avoided the sun and spent most of her time in the cellar where it was cool.

"Is there anything we can do for you?" Rosalyn asked her.

"Yes, anything at all, dear Melody?" Roddy added.

But the girl could think of nothing for them to do. She emerged from the cellar only under the cool light of the moon. As spring turned to summer, she grew weaker by the day. On midsummer's eve, a gaggle of children came to the door after dark and asked if Melody could join them in making a bonfire, something they did every year. Roddy and Rosalyn had reservations, but they couldn't resist their daughter's eagerness at the thought of participating in this important event. Melody kissed her parents goodbye and promised to be careful before scampering off with her friends.

During the celebration, she laughed and danced along, newly energized by everyone's laughter and good cheer. And when the bonfire was almost burned out, she watched as her friends took turns jumping over the flames. Some went alone, others in groups of two or three. She stood nearby, longing to leap, but uncertain she had the strength to do it. Then two of her friends took her hands and tugged.

They got a good running start, but alas, Melody's toe touched a flame as they crossed over. There was a hiss and a flicker. And in an instant the snow girl was gone. All that remained was a little water on the palms of the children who had touched her hands.

So Roddy and Rosalyn were once again without a child of their own. A few people said it was just as well because any snow child, no matter how charming, was the work of the devil. But nobody really believed that. And for the rest of their days, Roddy and Rosalyn reminisced about the daughter who had passed so briefly through their lives but left a lasting mark of love.

Notes on the Stories

The Frog Who Wouldn't Budge: This is an original tale I created for Aunt Truly to tell in my novel, *The Kiminee Dream*. I'm sure it was informed by stories I've heard and read over the years, but I didn't have a specific tale in mind when penning this one.

Milk for Grandma's Coffee: I came upon the story that inspired this in a collection of folktales I once owned but have now lost track of. I recall neither the name of the book nor its author. The structure of this story is very much like the version I read, but the text is original. It is a type of story called a chain tale or cumulative tale in which action or dialogue repeats and builds in some way as the story unfolds. Many such tales feature a series of animals or forces of nature, each more powerful than the last.

The Seamstress: Nancy Shimmel, a storyteller and educator who lives in the San Francisco Bay Area, transformed the Yiddish song "Hob Ikh Mir a Mantl" ("I Had a Little Overcoat") about a tailor who makes increasingly smaller items from pieces of cloth into the chain/formula tale "Just Enough to Make a Story," published in her book *Just Enough to Make a Story: A Sourcebook for Storytelling* published in 1978 by Sisters Choice Press. In this version, I've made the main character a widowed seamstress living in Illinois.

The Diamond: This story was inspired by "The Ruby," which I came across in *More Ready-to-Tell Tales from Around the World*, edited by David Holt and William Mooney and published by August House in 2005. The original tale is a parable from the Hindu tradition that acclaimed storyteller Jim May contributed to the Holt-Mooney collection.

The Wee Woman Who Lived in a Teapot: The first time I ran across this tale was in Margaret Real MacDonald's introductory storytelling book, *Ready to Tell Tales*. In MacDonald's version, the central character is a little old woman who lives in a vinegar bottle. She gave as her source *A Dictionary of British Folk-Tales*, edited by Katharine M. Briggs, Bloomington Indiana University Press, 1970. My version puts a wee woman in a teapot. The bones, but not the text, of this tale stick very much with MacDonald's interpretation.

Crimson: This is an original chain (cumulative) tale that, while influenced by many stories I've read and heard, doesn't follow any well-known tale that I know of.

Hidden Skin: This is inspired by a folktales that have been told for centuries in Ireland, Scotland and other Celtic cultures where stories about selkies, mythical creatures that resemble seals in the water but assume human form on land, are still told, sung and believed. In this version, I brought the lore to North America and to Aunt Truly's family, which takes it from folklore to fiction.

Taken: This is my interpretation of a folktale of the same name that I found in *Favorite Folk Tales From Around the World* by Jane Yolen and published by the Pantheon Fairy Tale and Folklore Library. The version in that book is short. I researched and expanded the tale into the story contained herein. All of the text, including the song, is my own. Changelings are a popular motif in Irish and Scottish folktales.

The Mermaid's Gift: I first heard this story told by John Boe, professor emeritus of English at U.C. Davis, in a storytelling class he co-taught with Ruth Stotter at Dominican University in California. He used simple props to enhance the story and was mesmerizing. I've since run across variations of the tale in other settings as well as on the internet. This is my adaptation.

The Snow Girl: This is my version of the well-known Russian folktale Snegurochka (The Snow Maiden). The first English translation of this story was done by T. Keane and published in *The Prose Tales of Alexander Pushkin*, London, 1894. In the original, the girl who comes into the life of a childless old couple is half human and half ice and snow.

Acknowledgments

Today, we can share stories numerous ways: social media, email, blogs, movies, television, podcasts, radio, print books, ebooks, audio books, text, interactive apps, and more. But nothing is quite like the first way people told stories: in person around campfires, during sacred ceremonies, by the hearth, in royal courts, at seasonal fairs or at inns along trade routes. To these people, the ones who created stories and kept them alive by word of mouth century after century, I feel immense gratitude. I am humbled to be one of their descendants.

My ancestors hailed primarily from Ireland, and given the Irish people's gift for language, I imagine storytellers were among those who came directly before me. I expect, for example, my great, great grandfather Patrick McHale—who was born in Ireland, came to America in his youth and later joined an Illinois Union regiment in the Civil War—could spin a story or two. But as each new generation took root here, the gift of story faded, and tales became truncated.

On my grandmother's knee, I heard anecdotes, not full stories, but they were so vivid I saw them unfold as she spoke, and I treasure those tidbits, for she told them with love.

Telling stories with love brings me to the late writer Brian Doyle. I was deeply moved by his novel, *Chicago*. I sensed within its chapters a subtext of love that profoundly affected the way I wrote my novel *The Kiminee Dream*, in which Aunt Truly is introduced as an enigmatic, healing storyteller.

When it comes time to give thanks, I think of Ruth Stotter for the work she has done for decades to promote live storytelling, encourage people to develop and keep the craft alive. She also reviewed the stories in this collection and added to my notes, making them far more accurate. Then there is my family: Jim, Ryan, Jack, Moira, Roger, Ava, Reina, Kathy and Mary Ruth. They are always with me and I with them as we wend our way through this increasingly complex world. And there are dear friends who have encouraged me at important junctures in life, in particular those who belong to Redwood Writers, the Sonoma County branch of the California Writers Club, as well as my long-time friend Holly Whitman who expertly copyedited this little volume.

To all of you, thank you so much.

Note to Readers

Thank you for taking time to read *Aunt Truly's Tales*. I sincerely hope you enjoyed it. When I began writing *The Kiminee Dream*, the novel that introduces Aunt Truly, I didn't know one of the characters would be a storyteller. She just showed up, uninvited. Now, it would be difficult to imagine the novel without her. Creating this new book of tales is a way to give her more dimension while sharing some of my favorite stories with you.

What about you? Do you have a favorite story in this collection? Or a least favorite? As an author, I love feedback. After all, you're the reason I continue to write. So please tell me what these stories did or didn't do for you by email to laura@WORDforest.com or via the contact form at http://lauramchaleholland.com.

Finally, I need to ask a favor. If you're so inclined, please post a review of *Aunt Truly's Tales* on your favorite online review sites. For independent authors, reviews are tough to come by, and you, the reader, have the power to make or break a book.

Thank you so much for reading *Aunt Truly's Tales* and for spending time with me.

In gratitude,
Laura McHale Holland

About Laura

In my work, I hunt for hope in unlikely places and often weave fantastic elements into stories grounded in reality. My books have received recognition in the indie publishing sphere, including the National Indie Excellence Awards, Next Generation Indie Book Awards, and Indies Book Awards. In addition, four of my short plays have been produced in Northern California, where I live with my husband and two goofy little mutts.

An avid fan of story performance, I also enjoy freeing stories from the printed (or digital) page. To learn more, please visit https://lauramchaleholland.com, where you can read blog posts and book excerpts, as well as join my community of readers, which will bring you a free flash fiction collection, previews of works in progress, members-only special offers and a dose of inspiration.

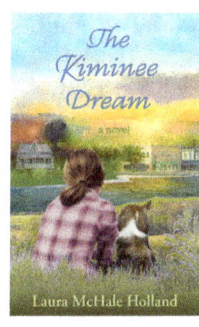

What people are saying about

The Kiminee Dream

"*Laura McHale Holland knows a thing or two about the beauty to be found in characters from America's heartland. They are always quirky and some are on magical, profoundly personal quests. And if their fellow travelers include pets, wildlife and even the landscape itself, it all makes for a hypnotic and endearing story. The turn of The Kiminee Dream's final page feels like the end of a much-needed visit home.*"

—Rayne Wolfe, former New York Times staff writer,
San Francisco Chronicle columnist, and author of *Toxic Mom Toolkit*

"*Richly written, full of magical realism and deeply atmospheric, The Kiminee Dream is as much a love letter to the interconnected lives of small town residents as it is a testament to how inexplicably linked our lives are, no matter how far removed.*"

—Kristin Fields, author of *A Lily in the Light*

"*One of the most impressive things for me was the lyrical quality of the storytelling, which flows both like poetry and fairytale as the plot unfolds with huge amounts of detail and atmosphere. Holland's pen crafts gorgeous images that represent the moods and ideas of the town and its characters, bathing them in shadow and light as different events play out. I felt* that the characters were also exceedingly well developed with keen attention to their attitudes and emotions, making for a richer sense of kinship and rivalry within the town itself."

—K.C. Finn for Readers Favorite

"More than a delightful visit to the heartland in a simpler time, it's easy to confuse The Kiminee Dream with a tale of Midwest charm and quirky characters—sure, it's got all that—but there are twists and turns that take you to a dark side that you don't see coming. Laura McHale Holland sheds the stereotypes (while still squeezing plenty of whimsy out of them) with a tale of larger than life characters in a small town."

—Ransom Stephens, author of *Too Rich to Die*

"The little town of Kiminee, Illinois, population 1,257, has always had something magical about it. Why, if you listen closely, you can even hear the Bendy River, which flows alongside this burg, burbling to the tune of "You Are My Sunshine." But the residents of Kiminee also have a few skeletons secreted away—both real and metaphorical. Cozy up with this novel when you have a few hours; Laura McHale Holland has crafted a page-turner. Once you enter this world, you won't want to leave until the last mystery is solved."

—Michel Wing, author of *Body on the Wall: Poems*

"This is an amazing lark of a novel. I have to admit, it took me more than one try, right at the start, because I was introduced to six characters in the first page or two. But I stuck with it, and thank heavens—the book is filled with unique characters I fell in love with and will remember for a long time: particularly Tam-Tam, Emily, and Buster—there is plenty of tension and mystery, and even some magical realism. I highly recommend this read."

—Skye Blaine, author of The Pensing Connection series

"While containing quite a bit of melodrama, The Kiminee Dream remains a deeply poetic and riveting novel, full of family secrets and the complex relationships right underneath the cheery façade of American normalcy."

—Royal Young for IndieReader

"*Laura McHale Holland is a consummate story teller and knows how to capture the essence of the human spirit. Her characters dance with magic and surprised me over and over again. The Kiminee Dream took me to a different place, yet somehow remained familiar and relatable. I thoroughly enjoyed this fun read, and strongly recommend it.*"

—**Anne E. Philipp, author of *Grand Theft Death***

"*This enchanting novel draws you in from the dramatic, mysterious prologue to the very last page. A town of characters develops before your eyes and welcomes you into their world. Intricate stories are woven together as painful pasts unravel. The Kiminee Dream reads like a contemporary fairy tale, and I finished the book ending up feeling like I had been part of its magic, and wishing for more.*"

—**Tanya Savko, author of *Enough to Go Around***

Excerpt from

The Kiminee Dream

Prologue

In the town of Kiminee, the end was never the end, sorrow left supple scars and wishes cracked reality. This was true back in January 1936, when a teenager forced too soon into womanhood darted through a moonlit winter night, exhaling moist clouds into biting air. Clad in a sleeveless, cotton nightgown and slippers worn thin, the young fan of radio dramas, black roses and Bing Crosby's mellow baritone didn't wince at the cold. She ran on, eyes glazed with fever, dewy skin blemished.

At the riverbank, she vaulted over snow-covered boulders onto solid ice. With arms outstretched and face tilted skyward, she glided. Voice wavering, she rasped a lullaby her mother used to sing in a city where coal dust muted the horizon. Her heart thrummed. Tears flowed. Blood slid down her thighs.

She kicked up her feet. Gone were the slippers, replaced by skates of purest-white leather with gleaming blades; gone was the nightie, replaced by a costume with sequined rainbows and silver fringe. She leaped, spun, landed. Ice cracked. She rose and fell again. The brittle surface groaned. She leaped higher, higher—each time a creak, a crack. Into the air she twirled once more. When she touched down, a fissure welcomed her. She plummeted, lips closed, eyes smiling.

When she embraced her maker that bleak Illinois night in the depths of the Great Depression, all residents of the community nestled along the river's curves were asleep. Except for one. And for decades to come, they knew nothing of her brief life and demise.

Except for one.

End of excerpt

www.ingramcontent.com/pod-product-compliance
Lightning Source LLC
Chambersburg PA
CBHW081919130726
47909CB00015B/3036